Burkhard Fries · Marcus Pfister

# THE RAINBOW FISH
## Classroom Companion

For school and kindergarten

North
South

First published in the United States, Great Britain, Canada, Australia,
and New Zealand in 2017 by NorthSouth Books Inc., an imprint of NordSüd Verlag AG,
CH-8005 Zürich, Switzerland.

Distributed in the United States by North-South Books Inc., New York 10017.

Library of Congress Cataloging-in-Publication Data is available.
Printed in Germany by Grafisches Centrum Cuno GmbH & Co. KG, Calbe, January 2017.
ISBN: 978-0-7358-4290-8
1 3 5 7 9 · 10 8 6 4 2
www.northsouth.com
www.rainbowfish.us
Meet Marcus Pfister at www.marcuspfister.ch

# INTRODUCTION

I love my job: developing new stories and characters, letting my creative imagination run free, and trying out new techniques and illustrations–it's all quite simply fun.

Of course I'm always delighted when I get nice responses to my work emails, letters, and drawings, etc. What gives me particular pleasure is when my books inspire readers to do something creative themselves. They might build or bake, paint a picture, or sing a song; and that is the best kind of praise I can get.

That is the reason why I am offering you some ideas and starting points with this little book. You can change or simplify whatever you find here, or make up new things. As long as you end up with something of your own, a drawing or a song or a little play you can perform, this book will have served its purpose. So good luck, and have fun!–*Marcus Pfister*

# CONTENTS

# 1 | DESIGNING A FISH

## Design a fish in 3 simple steps

★ Using pencils, ask children to draw a big fish.
  - As an alternative to drawing the fish, the outline of a fish (page 7) can be copied and may be easier for children who are not experienced at drawing.
  - Encourage children to add an eye, a mouth, fins, and scales to their drawings.
    (Scales can be made using U-shaped letters in rows.)

★ Once the pencil drawing is complete, ask the children to color the scales with wax crayons. (The Rainbow Fish can be used as a model, with colorful scales and plenty of silver scales.)

★ Now children can use a small sponge dipped in blue watercolor to color the fish and background.

🐟 TIP: Wax crayons will repel the water. The areas not colored with crayons will become the hue of the watercolor of their choice. Blue might be a nice choice for the background.

### MATERIALS

Drawing pad

Pencil, eraser

Crayons

Watercolor paints

Small sponge

Rainbow Fish book

# 2 | DESIGNING AN UNDERWATER WORLD

## Paint an underwater seascape in 3 easy steps!

★ Ask questions to stimulate the children's imaginations:
 - What plants grow on the seabed?
 - What shapes and colors do they have?

★ Using a small sponge and some watercolors, paint a bright, sandy seabed on the bottom half of a piece of paper. Then use the sponge to spread light blue over the top half of the page to represent the seawater. Let the painting dry.

★ After about 20 minutes, when the seabed is dry, the children can use wax crayons to draw colorful underwater plants, fish, and other sea creatures as well.

More questions to help stimulate creativity:
 - Where is the Rainbow Fish hiding?
 - Is that a submarine gliding past?
 - Might there be a reef or an underwater cave?
 - Maybe there's a treasure chest from a sunken pirate ship.

MATERIALS

Drawing pad
Small sponge
Watercolors
Crayons

# 3 | DRAWING TO (CLASSICAL) MUSIC

Encourage children to draw to the accompaniment of (classical) music. Afterward, they can color in what they have drawn.

★ Ask the children to sit or stand at a table with a drawing pad and pencil.

★ As soon as the music starts, they can begin to draw—expressing the sound of the music in their drawings. Play the music for 1 to 2 minutes.

★ Encourage the children to draw curves and waves keeping their pencils moving the whole time (without lifting the pencils off of the paper). (Gentle music might inspire children to draw large curves; more lively music might inspire them to draw small waves.)

★ When the music ends, ask the children to put down their pencils.

Ask the children to use their imagination to recognize shapes, waves, and patterns.

★ Now ask the children to color their creations using crayons, watercolors, or colored pencils.

## MATERIALS

Drawing pad

Crayons

Watercolors/colored pencils

Small sponge

CD player/Internet access

Music (Mozart: Horn Concerto no. 4; Vivaldi: "Spring," the Four Seasons; Schubert: 4 impromptus, D. 899 op. 90, no. 2 in E-Flat Major, for example)

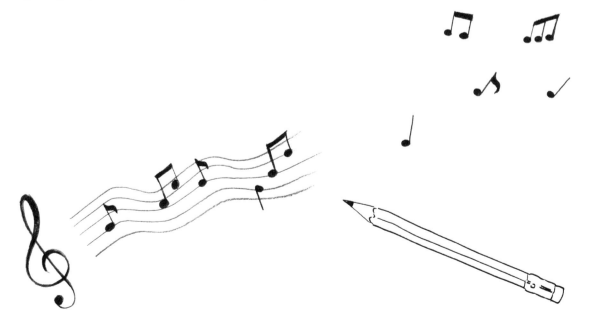

# 4 | SEWING A FISH ONTO CARDBOARD

## Sew the outline of a fish in 4 simple steps!

⭐ Ask children to draw a large fish (or glue a copy of the fish from page 7) onto a brightly colored piece of cardboard.

⭐ Using pencils, ask the children to mark the outline of the fish with dots for the stitching.
**TIP:** An even number of holes works best (10 to 20 holes would be great).

⭐ Ask children to puncture a hole in each "dot" using a hole punch or craft punch.
(The children can do this themselves using a suitable base.)

⭐ Using blunt needles, they can begin "sewing."
**TIPS:**
- If this is the children's first experience of sewing, it would be helpful to explain how to thread the needle: hold the thread in a little bow between the thumb and the tip of the index finger so that it can just be seen. Then the "hungry needle" can approach with its open mouth (O) and "eat" the thread.
- A simpler backstitch is more suitable for beginners. More advanced children can also work with backstitch, and if the edge is large enough they can use chain stitch.
- If you also want to create scales with stitches, you can sew triangles. It can all be made to look very attractive with threads of different colors or simply with silver.

### MATERIALS

Needle (blunt)

Pencils

Yarn, different colors

Hole punch or craft punch

Drawing of fish (copied) on cardboard

Optional: Glue

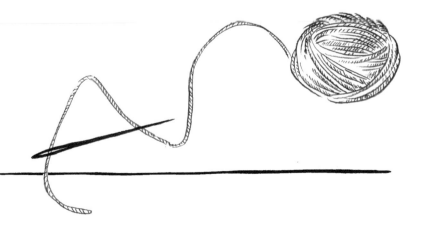

# 5 | MAKING YOUR OWN PLAY PIECES

## Make "play pieces" in 4 simple steps!

★ Ask the children to draw a character on a piece of cardboard. (Keep it small, like the size of an apple.) (It could be a character they make up or perhaps one of their favorite characters from *The Rainbow Fish*.)

★ Ask children to color both sides of their characters.

★ Then assist children in cutting them out using safety scissors.

★ Using a small piece of clay, children can create a "base" so that their character (play piece) can stand up. (The clay can be rolled into a ball and compressed so that it can stand firmly on the table without falling over.)
**TIP:** If the children design their own figures, make sure they are large enough and cut them out. If you use the models on page 13, it would be a good idea to copy the outlines or glue the drawings onto solid cardboard (120g/160g).

### MATERIALS

Template on page 13

Safety scissors

Colored pencils

Modeling clay

Cardboard (120g/160g)

Glue

## Let the fun begin!

- Encourage the children to have "free play" using their play pieces, making underwater plants or a boat made out of clay, a cave made from a shoe box, or a mountain made from a cloth, etc.
- Ask the children to act out a picture book story with their play pieces or develop a different story of their own.

# 6 | SHADOW PLAY

## Create a shadow play!

★ Ask children to draw a character on some cardboard, then color it in.

★ Assist children in cutting out their characters using safety scissors. If you use the models on page 13, it is best to copy or glue the figures onto solid cardboard (120g/160g).

★ Help children tape their characters to wooden (kebab) sticks with some tape.

★ The best light source is a digital or overhead projector or flashlight.

★ A white cloth hung on a clothesline will make a good screen.

★ The children-one for each figure-can start by playing any games they like. Later, they can be offered some sort of framework, as in the game with figures (see page 13).

🐟 **TIPS:** As an alternative, the white cloth can be hung over a table.
Place the light source behind the cloth.
Hold the play pieces in front of the light and behind the curtain. Have fun!

> ### MATERIALS
>
> Template on page 13
>
> Cardboard (120g/160g)
>
> Safety scissors
>
> Tape
>
> Thin wooden sticks (e.g., kebab skewers)
>
> Digital or overhead projector or flashlight
>
> Clothesline and clothespins
>
> Cloth
>
> Optional: Glue

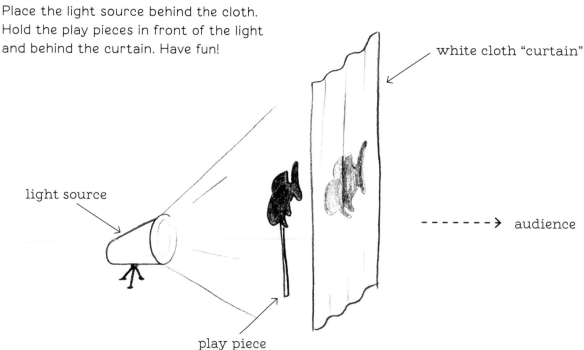

white cloth "curtain"

light source

- - - - - - → audience

play piece

13

# 7 | A LITTLE DANCE

## Move to the groove in this celebration of music and dance!

★ Distribute the words to the song.
Then ask the children to listen to the song
once or twice and learn the words.

★ Now, have fun dancing and moving to
the music and words!

🐟 **TIPS:** If possible, move desks and chairs back so
children have room to dance.
Encourage children to move to the song–swimming
to the left, then swimming to the right, and
flapping and shaking their "fins" and "tails!"

 MATERIALS

Worksheet with song lyrics:
"The Fish Dance" by E&E.

Internet access - the link to
this song can be found at
these websites:

www.northsouth.com

www.rainbowfish.us

Space to dance!

# THE FISH DANCE

All the little fishies in the deep blue sea
Swimming so wild and swimming so free
Moving to the beat and the melody
Won't you gather round all you little fishies
And do the fish dance with me

Swim to the left
Swim to the right
Flap your fins, shake your tail
Now you're feeling all right
Leap up high
Dive down low
Flap your fins, shake your tail
And that's how the fish dance goes!

All the little fishies in the deep blue sea
Dancing together joyfully
Moving to the beat and the melody
Big fish, small fish, starfish, shellfish
Do the fish dance with me!

Swim to the left
Swim to the right
Flap your fins, shake your tail
Now you're feeling all right
Leap up high
Dive down low
Flap your fins, shake your tail
And that's how the fish dance goes!

# 8 | MAKING A SIMPLE STOP-MOTION CARTOON

Make a simple stop-motion cartoon in 7 easy steps! Stop-motion is a lot like a "flip book," in which a series of images set in a swift sequence gives the illusion of the movement.

➤ **TIPS:**
- You can use a laptop with a webcam, an iPad, or a smart phone.
- You can use these free software programs to help you:
  MonkeyJam
  VSDC Free Video Edition–editing program
  Audacity–lets you add dialogue, sound effects, and music

MATERIALS

PC/laptop with webcam, or iPad or smart phone

Suitable apps (see instructions below)

Watercolors, paintbrush

Coloring pad

Safety scissors

Masking tape

★ Decide what your cartoon will be about. If you're working with young children, you won't need to create a storyboard (which is normally used in planning a film). You can simply discuss with the children whether you want to film a single scene or the whole picture book.

For example, if you want to show the Rainbow Fish looking for the octopus, think about which items or characters need to be moved, e.g., the Rainbow Fish and the octopus, and perhaps another fish as a supporting actor.

★ Draw, color, and cut out these characters (or use the materials created from the previous activities).

★ Create a background scene for children to make with watercolors (such as an underwater world with a cave).

★ When everything is ready–the background and the characters–discuss the basic sequence of events with the children:
How should the characters move? (For example, will the Rainbow Fish come from the left of the picture and swim around in a circle before he discovers the cave, or will he swim straight to it?)

🐟 TIP: Remind children that the steps must happen one at a time (that the characters will only move a few centimeters at a time for each still photo created).

★ Tape the background picture to the wall so that it won't slip when the children move the characters over it.

★ Divide children into small groups (two works best). Each group can work on a scene: one child moves the character, then puts her hand behind her back and gives the order "Capture." The other child can take the photograph. This goes on until the whole scene has been acted and photographed as planned.

★ Combine the scenes using the software of your choice.

🐟 TIPS:
- Ideally, five pictures will equal about one second of film. The more pictures you take per second, the smoother the animation. This can be adjusted according to the software you are using.

- With MonkeyJam, you can also add a soundtrack for dialogue and music. However, the length of this can't be varied. (If you are working with MonkeyJam, you will end up with a film in AVI format. You can use this for more editing programs. The advantage is that you can create several tracks–one for the film, one for the spoken text, one for sound effects, one for music, etc.)

- If you want to include music or sound effects and are working with an iPad, the app Garageband is very useful, especially because you will have access to a lot of freely available music of all styles.

- Children will gain a lot of practical experience in using different technologies.

# TIPS ON HOW TO HANDLE FEELINGS
## For Activities 9-13

Emotions can feel great, but sometimes they can make us feel overwhelmed. In these activities, children will review the names of different emotions, learn to become more aware of them, and explore how to express them.

The main feelings covered are happy (joy), sad (grief), mad (angry), and scared (fear). The children will learn how to distinguish between them and how to cope with them using acting and simple role-play.

**▶ TIPS FOR ACTIVITY 9:**
- Create a line on the floor (using masking tape or a jump rope). When the children cross the border, they can begin acting and playing a different character.

- After the role-play or the mime, you can start a short discussion in which the children describe what they felt. This is a chance for them to tell about similar experiences they have had in real life.

- This kind of play-acting may be too difficult for nursery school children, and the earliest one might start is ages 5 to 6.

# 9 | ACTING—MAKING "STATUES"

## Exploring emotions through acting and movement.

★ Whisper one of the four emotions in the child's ear (happy, sad, mad, or scared). Ask the child to act out the emotion in front of the other children. As a "statue," she adopts a suitable pose and then "freezes" when she thinks she has got it right. She now stands like a statue.

★ Ask the other children to guess the emotion and say it out loud when asked.

★ Different children then act as statues, expressing other emotions the others have to guess.

**MATERIALS**

Masking tape or jump rope

### Being an outsider/being different

★ A variation is for a group to act out a feeling while two children stand apart acting out a different (opposite) feeling. They can be separated from the others.

★ This can lead to a discussion:
  - How do you feel when you're left on your own like that?
  - Would you like to be in (go back into) the group?
  - Has anything like this ever happened to you in real life?
  To the group:
  - How did you feel being all together in a group?
  - Has anything like this ever happened to you in real life?
  - Which passage in the picture book corresponds to this "statue"?

★ This game can easily be made to fit in with the picture book. What parallels can you find?
  - How does the Rainbow Fish feel (in various parts of the book)?
  - What would you do if you were the other fish, or if you were the Rainbow Fish?

## Being proud/arrogant

★ When the children have lost their inhibitions–which they might when they start these games–you can make a direct reference to what happens in the picture book.

★ Ask a child to play the part of the Rainbow Fish adopting a proud, arrogant attitude. (This can be reinforced by folding the arms, holding the head high, and making dismissive gestures.)

★ Ask other children (about five, acting the parts of other fish) to "swim" around the first fish and try to come close. They can express their admiration and can try to touch the arrogant fish (perhaps they would like to have such silver scales). But he won't let them touch him and (coolly) fends them off.

★ Perhaps the other fish give up and start to ignore him–moving to the other side of the room. (This action can express the emotional side of the events and the Rainbow Fish's sense of isolation.)

# 10 | ACTING—"A JOURNEY TO THE ISLANDS OF EMOTION"

## Exploring emotions with acting and music!

★ Arrange the chairs on one side of the room in such a way that the children feel they are sitting in a big rowboat. Each child should be able to row easily with an (imaginary) oar. You can be the captain at the front or back of the boat.

★ The rest of the children are on the other side of the room on an (imaginary) island. This group is waiting for the boat to reach the island.

★ You and the children begin to "row" to the island.

★ Tell the children about the legend of the hidden Islands of Emotion that you and they are setting out to discover. The current is very strong, and they must row with all their strength to move forward.

★ At last you reach the hidden islands. The captain gives the order that everyone should climb very carefully out of the boat. As they do so, they all wonder which Island of Emotion they have landed on.

★ The secret of the island will only be revealed once the sailors come ashore. The behavior of the island inhabitants will let children know which emotion is being acted out as they move in time to the accompanying music.

★ As soon as the occupants of the boat step ashore, the music begins. All the natives move/dance in time to the (classical) music as they try to express one of the emotions.

---

### MATERIALS

Chairs (for half of the children)

CD player/Internet access

Classical music, e.g.,
- Edvard Grieg: "In the Hall of the Mountain King"
- Johann Sebastian Bach: Badinerie
- Edvard Grieg: "Solveig's Song"
- Nikolai A. Rimsky-Korsakov: "Flight of the Bumblebee"

★ The following pieces of music are simply suggestions–you are of course free to choose whatever you like:
-Island of Fear: Grieg: "In the Hall of the Mountain King"
-Island of Joy: Bach: Badinerie
-Island of Grief: Grieg: "Solveig's Song"
-Island of Anger: Rimsky-Korsakov: "Flight of the Bumblebee"

★ As soon as the music begins and the natives start dancing, it may happen that the explorers also feel the emotion and join in the dance. They should be allowed to do so, but it is also all right if an explorer prefers simply to watch.

★ After a while the music stops and the natives "freeze." Then the explorers say which emotion they think was being expressed. If the majority of them guess right, they can all go back to the boat.

★ The explorers sit down in the boat to continue their journey. They row to the next island, where they once more meet the (same) natives, but this time there are different movements and different music to express a different emotion.

★ This continues until all four islands have been explored. You can play the game again, switching the groups around, or you can repeat it on another day.

# 11 | A SONG OF DIFFERENCE

## A song to celebrate differences and working together!

★ Divide the children into 3 groups.
- Ask Group 1 to draw a picture of a <u>blue</u> starfish.
- Ask Group 2 to draw a picture of a <u>purple</u> starfish.
- Ask Group 3 to draw a starfish of <u>any color</u> they prefer.

★ Ask the children to listen to the song once or twice and learn the words.

★ Now, act it out!
- Ask Group 1 to sing the first verse while holding up their <u>blue</u> starfish drawings. Ask Group 2 to approach Group 1 (while holding their drawings of <u>purple</u> starfish).

- Ask Group 2 to sing the second verse while holding up their <u>purple</u> starfish drawings. Ask Group 1 to approach Group 2 (while holding their drawings of <u>blue</u> starfish).

- Now, ask Group 3 to sing the last verse while holding up their <u>any color</u> starfish drawings. Ask Groups 1 and 2 to approach Group 3 (while holding their drawings of <u>blue</u> and <u>purple</u> starfish).

- Finally, ask all groups to sing the last verse together!

★ Discussion: How does it feel to be accepted? How would it feel if you were turned away from joining the other starfish? Which world would you rather live in? Why?

➤ TIP: Encourage children to move to the song–waving their arms and shaking their legs, etc.

---

**MATERIALS**

Worksheet with song lyrics: "The Land of Starfish" by E&E.

Internet access–The link to this song can be found at these websites:
www.northsouth.com
www.rainbowfish.us

Paper

Crayons (blue, purple, and any other colors)

---

# THE LAND OF STARFISH

In the land of the blue starfish . . . everyone is blue
And if a purple starfish comes along . . . here's
what the blue starfish do
They say, we like purple, come and play!
You've brightened our rock on this sunny day.
Wave your arms, shake your legs–look at our
colorful bay!

In the land of the purple starfish . . . everyone is
purple
And if a blue starfish comes along . . . here's what
the purple starfish do
They say, we like blue, come and play!
You've brightened our rock on this sunny day.
Wave your arms, shake your legs–look at our
colorful bay!

In the lands of the wise starfish, everyone is wel-
come.
And when a new starfish comes along, here's what
the wise starfish say . . .
They say, welcome friends to this rainbow land
Join us here; come take our hand . . .
We can work together to make the world better
And brighter every day!
We can work together to make the world better
And brighter every day!

# 12 | A STANDING-UP GAME

## Learning about each other!

★ Ask the children to sit in a circle on the floor or on chairs.

★ Throughout the game, nobody except you will say a word. The only form of communication is standing up. When the children want to signal their agreement, they stand up in silence. After a moment or two they sit down again. Nobody has to stand up if they don't want to.

★ You can ask questions to test the reactions of the children. Each one will be preceded by the instruction:
- "Please stand up silently if . . .".

★ Start off with questions that are easy to answer, such as:
- "Please stand up silently if you like apples."
- "Please stand up silently if you like soccer."

★ Questions can be on the subject of friendship; for instance, there are certain questions that will touch on the children's individual experiences (see model examples on page 28).
Of course one can also focus on matters arising out of the makeup of the class itself.
- The purpose of the game is to show the children that they need not feel that their experiences are unique to themselves, but that others in their age group have the same feelings.
- The vocabulary used in the questions presupposes a certain degree of knowledge, e.g., terms such as "jealousy" and "envy." If necessary, one should explain them beforehand, perhaps using the picture book.

★ It is also possible to keep the questions general and simply to relate them to the experiences of the Rainbow Fish in the picture book. Then the situation is not quite so delicate since the children are not directly talking about their experiences.

MATERIALS

Chairs to put in a circle

A list of instructions
(see worksheet on page 28)

# 🐟 Please stand up silently if . . .

. . . you like pizza.

. . . you like spinach.

. . . you like soccer.

. . . you like math.

. . . you like books.


. . . your friends have ever refused to let you play with them.

. . . you have ever felt left out.

. . . you have ever been envious because there was something you were not allowed to have.

. . . you have ever felt jealous of another child.

. . . you have ever felt lonely and abandoned.


. . . you have ever felt very sad.

. . . you have ever felt as if you don't know what to do.

. . . you have ever asked someone for help or advice.


. . . you have ever shared something with someone else, e.g., candy.

. . . you have ever shared something, even though you found it hard to do so.

. . . you have ever shared something, and afterward it made you feel good.

. . . you have ever shared something and have then realized that this made other people happy.


Space for your own ideas that might be useful for a particular group:

......................................................................................................

......................................................................................................

......................................................................................................

......................................................................................................

......................................................................................................

# 13 | A SONG OF SHARING

Giving is as fun as receiving! Celebrate sharing
with art and music.

 Part 1 (Making something to give)
- Give everyone a piece of paper and access to
  finger paints (or crayons).
- Ask each child to coat one of their hands in
  the paint color of their choice.
- Press your painted hand on the piece of paper
  to make a handprint. (If you're using crayons,
  ask children to trace an outline of their hand with
  a crayon on a piece of paper. Make sure to go in
  between each finger.)
- Now add eyes and a smile. (The palm can be
  the face of the fish. The fingers can be the fins.)
- Let the fish pictures dry (if necessary).

 Part 2 (Giving and receiving)
- Distribute the words to the song.
- Ask the children to listen to the song once or
  twice and learn the words.
- At the end of the song when the words say:
  "Give! Receive! Give! Receive! Give! Receive!"

- Ask children to give one of their paintings to
  someone in the class and to receive a drawing from
  someone else to experience "giving" and "receiving"

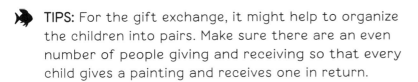 **TIPS:** For the gift exchange, it might help to organize
the children into pairs. Make sure there are an even
number of people giving and receiving so that every
child gives a painting and receives one in return.

MATERIALS

Finger paints or crayons

Paper

Worksheet with song lyrics:
"Sharing Feels Good"
by Paul Helou

Internet access-the link to
this song can be found
at these websites:
www.northsouth.com
www.rainbowfish.us

# SHARING FEELS GOOD

CHORUS

Sharing feels good when it comes from the heart

let's all get together let's all do our part

to give and receive just go ahead and start

sharing feels good when it comes from the heart


Giving and receiving makes the world go round

open up your heart, keep your feet on the ground

we share this Earth, we are one big family

I share with you and you share with me


CHORUS

You can share your things and share your company

give and let go, it makes you feel so free

when you share your heart, that's a lovely thing to do

when you shine your light, your light shines back at you


BRIDGE

You have the power to shine on everyone

Your heart is like a flower, your love is like the sun

So let love flow

Cause that's how your heart grows


CHORUS

The sun shines light on the Earth below

The soil drinks the rain, so the tall trees grow

The earth grows food for all of us to live

We share the food and smile as we give


Give! Receive! Give! Receive! Give! Receive!

# 14 | A GAME OF PERCEPTION

## Acting out the part of the Rainbow Fish!

★ Using a scarf, gently cover the child's eyes. Ask the child to pretend to be the Rainbow Fish and "swim" blindly from one side of the room to the other.

★ She must take care not to stop anywhere and not to bump into anything. There are lots of flora and fauna all around her.

★ Other children stand around in the room, holding different percussion instruments. They beat these whenever the Rainbow Fish comes too close to them. In this way, the various sounds serve to direct the Rainbow Fish.

★ Suitable background music can be played during the game (underwater theme).

★ Of course the children can then take turns to be the fish. Those with percussion instruments can also swap them and can take up different positions in the room.

★ Questions to start a discussion on personal space:
 - What is the difference between someone you like and someone you don't like?
 - What are your personal limits?

MATERIALS

A cloth or scarf to cover the eyes

Percussion instruments

Possibly background music (e.g., Saint-Saëns's *Carnival of the Animals*)

# HOW TO READ A PICTURE BOOK ALOUD

This section offers general tips on how to read (picture) books aloud.

★ If you want to read a (picture) book aloud, first you should create a relaxed, quiet, and comfortable atmosphere (a cozy corner, a sofa, floor cushions, a circle of chairs). Children who have had little or no experience of reading, and live in social conditions that are not conducive to reading, may need more time to accept being read to and to sit through an entire reading. You will probably need plenty of patience (keep cool!). Basically, though, all children are well disposed toward stories, whether told or read to them.

★ It goes without saying that if there are pictures, they should be visible to all the children so that they can follow the story line. If they are sitting in a circle, you can put the book on a music stand and read from it.

If the pictures are in digital form, you can use a digital projector or TV. Then the children will feel they are sitting in front of a screen in a kind of picture book movie theater.

★ When you are reading aloud, it is good to vary your voice, using highs and lows and different speeds. You can also use different voices for the individual characters, though that is not essential, especially if there are lots of them. That is best left to audio books with professional actors.

★ When there are particularly important passages in the text, you can pause to leave time for the children to make suggestions or to ask questions. This makes the reading into a kind of text interpretation, and you and the children can also make sure they are following the action.

You can also signal to them when there is a passage you want to read without interruption.

You should work out beforehand which parts of the text are suitable for a break. These will be passages that encourage the children to talk about their own personal experiences or that might make them speculate about how the story will go on.

# 15 | RECOGNIZING THE ORDER OF EVENTS IN A STORY

This activity helps children how to think about the order of events in a story and to reproduce it.

★ Describe and explain each of the illustrations.

★ Let the children talk about the sequence in which the pictures should be arranged. This can be done in pairs or in small groups.

★ The children then put the pictures together in the right order and number them.

★ Once a child has learned about writing and the written word, she can try to write individual words (e.g., *FISH*) that correspond to what is in the picture. With these first attempts to transcribe the spoken word, spelling is of secondary importance. The main thing is to give the child her first insight into the principles of the written language and so to encourage her to go on writing.

**MATERIALS**

Worksheet
(template on page 34)
Colored pencils

# Recognizing the order of events in a story

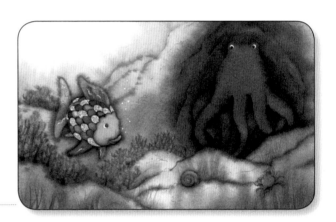

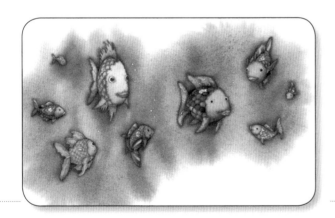

# 16 | READING WORDS

Reading, drawing, and matching!

The worksheet can be extended through reading activities.

★ The words are written in capitals for readability.

★ The children can also do reading exercises.

🐟 **TIP:** To make the reading easier, you can split longer words into syllables.

MATERIALS

Worksheet (on page 36)

Colored pencil

# 🐟 Reading at word level

1. Read and Draw.

| ✏️ | ✏️ | ✏️ | ✏️ |
|---|---|---|---|
| A FISH | AN OCTOPUS | A CAVE | A SCALE |

2. Read and Draw.

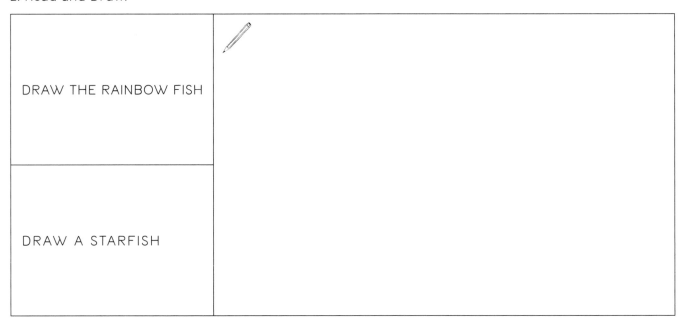

| DRAW THE RAINBOW FISH | ✏️ |
|---|---|
| DRAW A STARFISH | |

3. Matching! Draw a line from the word to the correct picture.

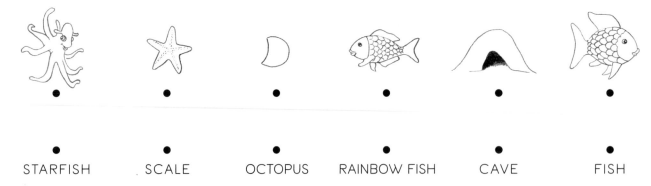

STARFISH  .SCALE  OCTOPUS  RAINBOW FISH  CAVE  FISH

# 17 | UNDERSTANDING THE STORY LINE

In this exercise the children can think about the sequence of events.

★ Ask children to read the simple sentences and match them to the corresponding pictures. In this way they can understand and think about the story line.

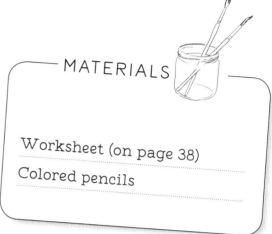

MATERIALS

Worksheet (on page 38)

Colored pencils

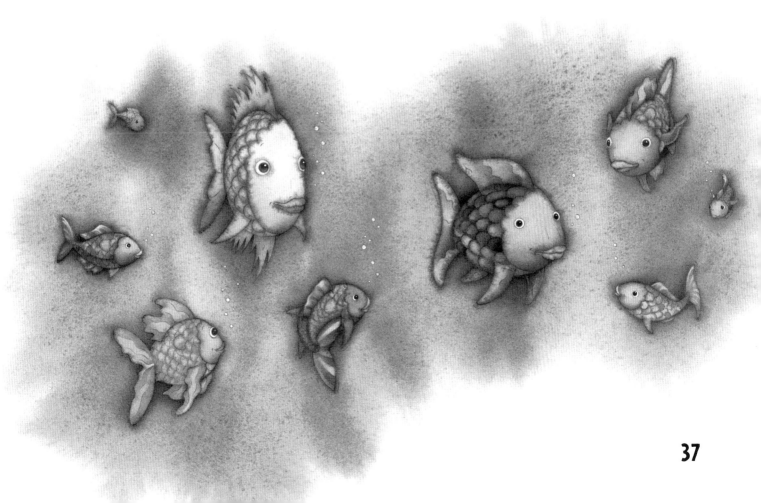

# 🐟 Understanding the story line 1

1. Put these sentences in the right order:

| 1 | THE RAINBOW FISH SWIMS PROUDLY THROUGH THE SEA. |
|---|---|
|   | THE RAINBOW FISH SHARES HIS GLITTERSCALES WITH EVERYONE. |
|   | THE RAINBOW FISH DRIVES THE LITTLE BLUE FISH AWAY. |
|   | ALL THE OTHER FISH TURN THEIR BACKS ON THE RAINBOW FISH. |
|   | THE RAINBOW FISH ASKS THE OCTOPUS FOR ADVICE. |
|   | THE RAINBOW FISH TAKES NO NOTICE OF THE OTHER FISH. |
|   | THE RAINBOW FISH IS LONELY AND SAD. |
| 8 | THE RAINBOW FISH HAS SHARED HIS SCALES WITH EVERYBODY AND IS HAPPY AGAIN. |

2. Match these pictures with the appropriate sentences:

      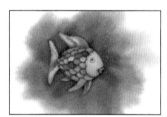

●　　　　　　　●　　　　　　　●　　　　　　　●

●　　　　　　　●　　　　　　　●　　　　　　　●

The little blue fish
is driven away.

The octopus gives
the Rainbow Fish
some advice.

The Rainbow Fish
shares his
glitterscales.

The Rainbow Fish
is lonely and sad.

3. Difficult words. Practice reading these words until you can do so without stumbling over them.

Rainbow Fish          coral reef            rainbow

glitterscale          octopus's cave        scaly robe

seabed                starfish              rainbow colors

# ⬛➤ Understanding the story line II

1. Complete the following sentences:

At first the Rainbow Fish is ●

● . . . kind.
● . . . proud.
● . . . friendly.

Then the Rainbow Fish realizes that ●

● . . . it's better to share.
● . . . sharing is stupid.
● . . . sharing makes everyone happy.

In the end the Rainbow Fish is ●

● . . . sad.
● . . . happy.
● . . . no longer lonely.

2. What happens in this chapter? Put a check mark next to YES or NO.

| | YES | NO |
|---|---|---|
| THE RAINBOW FISH DOESN'T NOTICE THE OTHER FISH. | | |
| THE RAINBOW FISH DOESN'T GIVE ANY GLITTERSCALES TO THE LITTLE BLUE FISH. | | |
| THE LITTLE BLUE FISH DOESN'T TELL THE OTHERS. | | |
| THE OTHER FISH LIKE PLAYING WITH THE RAINBOW FISH. | | |
| THE RAINBOW FISH GETS LONELIER AND LONELIER. | | |
| AT FIRST THE RAINBOW FISH DOESN'T EVEN SEE THE OCTOPUS. | | |
| LATER THE RAINBOW FISH REALIZES THAT IT'S NICE TO SHARE. | | |
| THE RAINBOW FISH GETS NO PLEASURE OUT OF SHARING. | | |
| IN THE END THEY ALL PLAY TOGETHER AGAIN. | | |

3. What do you think of the Rainbow Fish's behavior? Write it down.

........................................................................................................................................

........................................................................................................................................

........................................................................................................................................

........................................................................................................................................

# 18 | WRITING A LETTER OF COMPLAINT

Write a letter of complaint to the Rainbow Fish
on behalf of the little blue fish.

⭐ Read the picture book aloud to the point where the
little blue fish is driven away by the Rainbow Fish
and is not given a glitterscale.

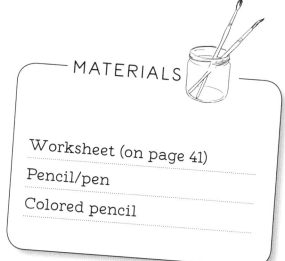

MATERIALS

Worksheet (on page 41)

Pencil/pen

Colored pencil

⭐ Stop reading and ask:
- How does the Rainbow Fish behave?
- How does the little blue fish feel now?
- What can the little blue fish do now?
- Imagine that the little blue fish could write
  and send a letter of complaint to
  the Rainbow Fish. What would he write?

⭐ If the children are not used to writing by themselves or find it difficult to express
themselves, you can tell them or suggest how to start some sentences:
- "I don't think its fair if . . ."
- "If you give me a glitterscale . . ."

⭐ The child can finish the letter by drawing something for the Rainbow Fish.

# 🐟 Writing a letter of complaint

Imagine you are the little blue fish. The Rainbow Fish just refused to give you a glitterscale.
Write a letter of complaint to the Rainbow Fish.

Dear Rainbow Fish,

# 19 | CHOOSING A DIFFERENT ACTION

Here you can show the children how to work out alternative actions and reactions. This is possible at several places in the picture book.

Read the picture book aloud and stop at the following places:

★ The little blue fish is driven away by the Rainbow Fish and tells the other fish all about it.
- What could the little blue fish have done instead?

★ The Rainbow Fish complains to the starfish about how unhappy he is. The starfish sends him to the cave of the octopus.
- What could the starfish have done instead?

★ The octopus gives the Rainbow Fish a piece of advice.
- What different advice could the octopus have given the Rainbow Fish?

🐟 TIP: After you have discussed the alternatives during these breaks, you can give out the worksheet and let the children tackle it. However, if you prefer to go step by step, you can cut the worksheet into sections and let the children write before you read aloud each new passage.

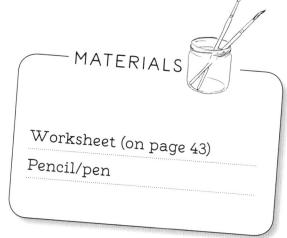

MATERIALS

Worksheet (on page 43)
Pencil/pen

# 🐟 Offering alternative courses of action

1. At first the little blue fish does not get any glitterscales from the Rainbow Fish.
   He tells all the other fish.
   - What could the little blue fish have done instead?

2. The Rainbow Fish complains to the starfish.
   The starfish tells him to go to the cave of the octopus.
   - What could the starfish have done instead?

3. The octopus gives the Rainbow Fish some advice.
   - What could the octopus have done instead?

# 20 | DESCRIBING ONE'S OWN EXPERIENCES

There are parallels here with Activity 12, the Standing-Up Game. The children can describe their own experiences, either orally or in writing. In this way they create a link with their own life and world.

★ Create a friendly atmosphere to give the children confidence. Tell them that (once again) this will be about their personal experiences and you would be pleased if one of them would be willing to share them with the class.

★ Make it clear that under no circumstances should any child be laughed at because of her experiences, because it is a brave child who is able to tell others about such private matters.

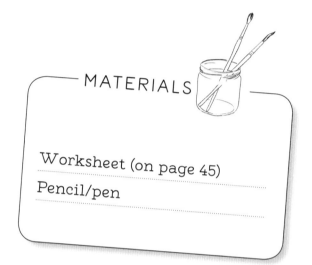

MATERIALS

Worksheet (on page 45)

Pencil/pen

# 🐟 Describing one's own experiences

1. Put a check mark next to things you have experienced.

○ My friends wouldn't allow me to play with them.
○ I've felt left out.
○ I've wanted something I wasn't allowed to have.
○ I've envied another person.
○ I've felt lonely and abandoned.

○ I've felt very sad.
○ I haven't known what I should do.
○ I've asked somebody for help or advice.

○ I've shared something, e.g., candy.
○ I've shared something even though I found it difficult to do so.
○ I've shared something and then I felt good.
○ I've shared something and then I've seen that it made others happy.

2. If you like, you can write about an experience you have had.

# ANSWERS

Understanding the story line I

| | |
|---|---|
| 1 | THE RAINBOW FISH SWIMS PROUDLY THROUGH THE SEA. |
| 7 | THE RAINBOW FISH SHARES HIS GLITTERSCALES WITH EVERYONE. |
| 3 | THE RAINBOW FISH DRIVES THE LITTLE BLUE FISH AWAY. |
| 4 | ALL THE OTHER FISH TURN THEIR BACKS ON THE RAINBOW FISH. |
| 6 | THE RAINBOW FISH ASKS THE OCTOPUS FOR ADVICE. |
| 2 | THE RAINBOW FISH TAKES NO NOTICE OF THE OTHER FISH. |
| 5 | THE RAINBOW FISH IS LONELY AND SAD. |
| 8 | THE RAINBOW FISH HAS SHARED HIS SCALES WITH EVERYBODY AND IS HAPPY AGAIN. |

2. Match these pictures with the appropriate sentences:

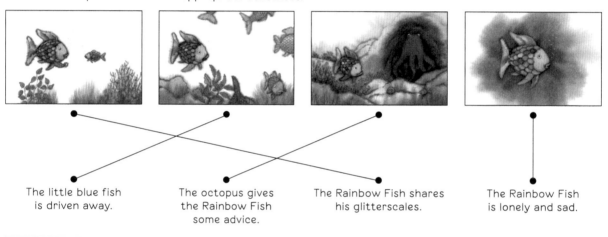

The little blue fish is driven away.

The octopus gives the Rainbow Fish some advice.

The Rainbow Fish shares his glitterscales.

The Rainbow Fish is lonely and sad.

## Understanding the story line II

At first the Rainbow Fish is . . . proud.

Then the Rainbow Fish realizes that . . . it's better to share.

In the end the Rainbow Fish is . . . happy. / . . . no longer lonely.

2. What happens in this chapter? Put a check mark next to YES or NO.

| | YES | NO |
|---|---|---|
| THE RAINBOW FISH DOESN'T NOTICE THE OTHER FISH. | X | |
| THE RAINBOW FISH DOESN'T GIVE ANY GLITTERSCALES TO THE LITTLE BLUE FISH. | X | |
| THE LITTLE BLUE FISH DOESN'T TELL THE OTHERS. | | X |
| THE OTHER FISH LIKE PLAYING WITH THE RAINBOW FISH. | | X |
| THE RAINBOW FISH GETS LONELIER AND LONELIER. | X | |
| AT FIRST THE RAINBOW FISH DOESN'T EVEN SEE THE OCTOPUS. | X | |
| LATER THE RAINBOW FISH REALIZES THAT IT'S NICE TO SHARE. | X | |
| THE RAINBOW FISH GETS NO PLEASURE OUT OF SHARING. | | X |
| IN THE END THEY ALL PLAY TOGETHER AGAIN. | X | |

# SOURCES

**Marcus Pfister** was born in Bern, Switzerland, in 1960. His great breakthrough as a picture book author came in 1992, when *The Rainbow Fish* took the bestseller list by storm. To date more than thirty million copies of the different volumes and editions have appeared all over the world in about fifty languages. In his studio, which has a fine view over Switzerland's capital city, Marcus Pfister continues to create more and more new characters and stories.

**Burkhard Fries** was born in 1969, and for many years he has lived and worked as a primary schoolteacher in Mannheim, Germany. He loves adapting literary texts for use in primary schools and is a keen creator of teaching materials for several different publishing firms.

**E&E** is singer/songwriter Eleanor Kleiner and multi-instrumentalist Elie Brangbour. Based in Beacon, New York, they also record and perform as The Whispering Tree, a Franco/American folk/rock duo.

**Paul Helou** is an award-winning songwriter, journalist, and actor. His CD for children, *Bears, Bees & Butterflies,* has won a Parents' Choice Award, among others. As a journalist, he has written feature articles for *The New York Times* and other publications. As an actor, Paul has appeared in regional theater and independent films. For more information, feel free to visit www.paulhelou.com.